TIGER'S TALE

Written by Michaela Morgan
Illustrated by Debbie Boon

1 Tiger

Tiger was not a very special cat. He had no particular talents and he lived nowhere in particular, but he could settle down anywhere ...
anywhere at all.

He perched in tall trees beneath the stars.
He snoozed on the hot tops of cars.

He lounged in sunny spaces in the park
and prowled on rooftops in the dark.

Yes, Tiger could settle anywhere.

3

But he did have his favourite places. One of them
was the library.

Every morning when the librarian arrived at
work, she would find Tiger on the doorstep.

She'd unlock the library door and he would pad in
and make himself at home.

The librarian liked Tiger. He helped to keep all her papers in place.

He helped to hold the door open.

Sometimes he helped to keep out the cold winds.
So the librarian was happy to have Tiger in the library.

And Tiger was happy to be in the library. It was cosy off the street. There were soft carpets and chairs to lie on. There were sunny spots to snooze in and he could listen to stories.

Sometimes the librarian read stories to the children. Sometimes the children read stories to each other. Some of the children read stories to themselves.

Tiger loved stories.
He would lie and snooze and dream and the stories
would tiptoe into his dreams. Then he would add
little bits of himself to each story.

2 "Tell us a story!"

Every evening when the library closed, Tiger would
go back out into the street and meet the cats that
lived there. They would have adventures. They would
sing songs. Sometimes they would have fights ...
and sometimes they would tell stories.

But two of the cats were special cats.
They could tell stories.

The Old, Old Cat had lived long and well.
She had seen so much and remembered so much.
She told tales of Long Ago.

Long, long ago, when I was no more than a fluffy kitten, there was a monster. His head was as big as a shed. His feet were like frying pans. His eyes glowed red in the night ...

Then there was the Ship's Cat. He had travelled far and wide. He had seen so much and remembered so much. He told tales of Far Away.

Far, far away and over the seas, there is a land where the trees talk to you ...

Tiger had not lived long. Tiger had not travelled far.
So he loved to hear these stories.

"Tell us another story!" he would say.

"Yes, tell us another story!" said the other cats.

"Please," Tiger begged. "Please, please, please,
P-L-E-A-S-E!"

But the Old, Old Cat said, "Not now, my dears.
I get tired. Time for my snooze."

And the Ship's Cat said, "Not now, me hearties.
I'm off on another swashbuckling adventure!
No more stories from me tonight."

Tiger sighed. "Never mind," he thought.
"I might hear another story tomorrow at the library."

13

So the next morning, bright and early, Tiger was waiting at the library door.

He dozed in a sunny corner inside. And all day long stories crept into his dreams.

Tiger was dreaming so happily and dozing so deeply that he didn't notice the librarian putting all the books away.

14

He didn't notice the librarian picking up her bag …
and getting her keys … and locking the door
behind her.

He didn't notice until it was too late.

3 Tiger turns a page

Tiger didn't panic. He'd been locked in before, so he wasn't frightened. He knew he would be all right.

There were many tasty mice to be caught in the library. There was plenty of water to drink. There were soft spots to snooze in and soon the librarian would be back to unlock the door.

But she didn't come back.

Closed
for holidays.
See you soon!

17

Tiger could keep himself busy for hours.
He could climb and jump and play.

18

But after a while he got bored.

There were no stars to stare at ... no moon
to sing to ... no one to fight with ... and no one
to tell him stories.

He stared at the books. "How do you get the stories
out of them?" Tiger wondered.

He tried licking a book to see if he could get the taste of a story. All that happened was the corner of the book got wet. So that didn't work.

Then he tried chewing a book to see if he could get the flavour of a story. That didn't work either.

Tiger stared and stared. He waited for the story to move so that he could pounce on it and catch it like a mouse.

But the book just lay still and quiet.

Tiger sighed deeply.
"AAAAH ...."
As if by magic, a page turned over.

"I remember that picture," thought Tiger.
"That's the Big Bad Wolf and he's saying "I'll huff and
I'll puff and I'll blow your house down."

Tiger turned the page with a careful paw. He looked
at the picture.
"I remember that," he said to himself. "That's where
the house blew down."

Tiger stared as only a cat can stare. He stared and
stared and wondered and wondered.

All that night, Tiger flicked through the pages
of the book. He looked at the pictures.
He told himself the bits of the story he
could remember.

The hours passed ...

and the night passed ...

and the days passed ...

... and still Tiger puzzled.

And ... bit by bit ...
... it all started to make sense.

4 A very special cat

Then there was no stopping him.
He read *The Cat in the Hat*.
He read *Puss in Boots*. He read *Mog*.
He read all sorts of stories.
He read and he read and he read.

The days and the nights passed quickly and soon
the librarian was back from her holiday.

At last, Tiger could go out at night to sit on his favourite wall.

The Ship's Cat told a tale of Far Away. The Old, Old Cat told a tale of Long Ago. But when all the other cats said, "Tell us another!" it was Tiger who told them a story ... and then another ... and another ... and another.

Tiger could tell all sorts
of stories now. He could
tell tales of Long Ago
and Far Away. He could
tell tales of Here and
Now. He could tell fairy
stories. He could tell
scary stories. He could
tell funny stories!

"Tiger, you really are something special!"
said all the other cats.
"You're a very talented cat."

Now, everyone knows that Tiger is a particularly special, particularly talented cat.

Tiger is a snoozer in the sun and a singer in the night. He's a cunning prowler and a midnight howler and he's the only cat that has ever learnt to read.

He's a **very** special cat indeed!

Ideas for guided reading

Learning objectives: use a variety of cues when reading; to notice the difference between spoken and written forms through re-telling known stories; to express views about a story, identifying specific words and phrases to support viewpoint; present and retell well-known stories.

Curriculum links: Citizenship; Taking Part; Living in a Diverse World.

Interest words: particular, prowled, librarian, adventures, special, travelled, hearties, swashbuckling, frightened, flavour, pounce, remember, talented

Word count: 1,145

Resources: whiteboard and pens

Getting started

This book can be read over two guided reading sessions.

- Introduce the book using its cover. Ask why 'Tiger's Tale' is a clever title ('tale' is a homonym with 'tail'). Ask the children to suggest some other homonyms (*there* and *their*, *been* and *bean*).

- Look at the front cover together. Who is Tiger? Discuss what could be happening in the story Tiger is telling. Introduce the word 'talents' and ask children what talents they have. Ask what talents Tiger might have and list them on the whiteboard.

- Ask the children to scan through up to p9, and discuss what other characters appear and the settings used in the story.

Reading and responding

- Return to the beginning of the first chapter. Dwell on interest words, for example, *particular, prowled*. Model using a range of strategies to read these words such as decoding and reading around the word, and discuss which strategy is the most useful.

- Read pp8–9 together. Look at the speech bubble on p9 closely. Ask for a volunteer to read this with appropriate expression.

- Ask the children to read silently to the end of p29, concentrating on reading speech bubbles and dialogue with expression. Listen to each child reading and praise good use of expression.